First published by Parragon in 2012

Parragon
Queen Street House
4 Queen Street
Bath BA1 1HE, UK

ISBN 978-1-4454-6484-8

Printed in China

MAGICAL STORY

Adapted by Lisa Marsoli

Illustrated by Caroline LaVelle Egan, Scott Tilley,
Andrew Phillipson, and Seung Beom Kim

Bath · New York · Singapore · Hong Kong · Cologne · Delhi
Melbourne · Amsterdam · Johannesburg · Auckland · Shenzhen

Finn McMissile, a British secret agent, had slipped onto an oil derrick. He was spying on a spectacled criminal named Professor Z.

Finn hid in the rafters and took photos of a TV camera. He also saw another secret agent who had been crushed into scrap metal!

Back in Radiator Springs, race car Lightning McQueen was at the Wheel Well Restaurant. Miles Axlerod – a former oil tycoon – and Italian race car Francesco Bernoulli were on TV. Axlerod was hosting an international race called the World Grand Prix to introduce his new alternative fuel, Allinol. Lightning agreed to join the race.

Lightning and his pit crew soon arrived in Tokyo for the first race. Mater embarrassed Lightning at the welcome party. He even leaked oil beside Axlerod.

Mater raced off to the bathroom. Inside the automated cubicle, he got poked, prodded and splashed with water!

While Mater was in the cubicle, two members of
Professor Z's crew, Grem and Acer, roughed up
American Agent Rod "Torque" Redline. When Mater
came out of the cubicle, Torque secretly stuck a
device underneath Mater.

The following day at the racetrack, Finn and his fellow agent, Holley Shiftwell, kept a close eye on Mater. They thought he was a secret agent, too!

Nearby, Grem and Acer aimed the TV camera at a race car. The camera was a weapon! Seconds later, the car's engine exploded. Some thought Allinol was to blame.

Professor Z's gang then went after Mater in the pits. They wanted the device that the American agent had planted on him.

Just as the bad cars were closing in on Mater, Finn rushed in to the rescue. Mater thought he was watching a karate demonstration!

Since Mater was distracted, he gave Lightning bad racing tips. Lightning ended up losing the race to Francesco!

Lightning blamed Mater. "I lost the race because of you!" he exclaimed.

Mater felt so terrible he decided to go back home. But Finn and Holley whisked him off on a spy mission instead.

Holley removed the planted device from Mater and found a photo of a mysterious, gas-guzzling engine. Mater noticed it had Whitworth bolts, which were very difficult to unscrew.

Meanwhile, Lightning and his team were just outside Porto Corsa, Italy visiting Luigi and Guido's hometown. Lightning talked to Luigi's Uncle Topolino about his fight with Mater.

"Everybody fights now and then, especially best friends," said Uncle Topolino. "But you gotta make up fast."

Holley, Finn and Mater were also on their way to Porto Corsa. Mater had told them the mysterious engine belonged to a Lemon – a car that didn't work right. They soon found out that a secret meeting of Lemons was being held in Porto Corsa. Holley disguised Mater as one of the Lemons' tow trucks so he could sneak into the meeting. She also gave him lots of spy gadgets!

Mater was soon in a room with Professor Z and all the Lemons. Then their "Big Boss", whose identity was hidden, appeared on a TV screen. He told the Lemons that once Allinol was proven dangerous, all cars would go back to using gasoline. Then the Lemons, who owned most of the world's oil, would become wealthy and powerful.

Outside, the second race had begun. Grem and Acer were on a nearby tower with the camera. They aimed it at the race car from Brazil. Her engine suddenly exploded!

Finn raced to the tower to stop Grem and Acer – but a helicopter captured him with a giant magnet!

Back at the race, Lightning crossed the finish line first! He then announced that he would still be using Allinol in the final World Grand Prix race in London.

The Big Boss heard this and gave the order to get rid of Lightning. Mater used his parachute to escape from the meeting. But before he could warn Lightning, Mater was kidnapped by the Lemons. They had captured Holley, too!

Finn, Holley and Mater were tied up inside the clockworks of Big Bentley in London. Mater finally convinced Finn and Holley that he wasn't a spy.

After the final race began, Grem and Acer told Mater they had planted a bomb inside Lightning's pit. As soon as the Lemons left, Mater escaped, racing to save his best friend.

Minutes later, Holley and Finn escaped, too. They soon discovered the Lemons had actually planted the bomb on Mater! Finn radioed the tow truck to tell him, but Mater was already in the pits.

"Stay away from me!" Mater warned Lightning.

But Lightning still raced forwards to see his best friend!

Meanwhile, Professor Z tried to escape on a combat ship, but Finn stopped him. He tied the Professor up in cables and brought him to Holley, Mater and Lightning.

Then Guido tried to remove the bomb on Mater, but he couldn't unscrew the bolts. Suddenly, everything made sense to Mater. He knew who the Big Boss was!

Mater flew with Lightning to Buckingham Palace. Mater told everyone that Axlerod was the Big Boss! Mater had figured it out because the bolts on the bomb were the same Whitworth bolts from the old British engine in the photo. The engine belonged to Axlerod. He was the biggest Lemon of all! Axlerod deactivated the bomb and everyone was saved.

The Queen thanked Mater by making him a knight!

Not long after Lightning got back home, he decided to hold his own "Radiator Springs Grand Prix". He invited all the international race cars. The whole town turned up for the race.

Finn and Holley showed up, too. They had come to invite Mater on their next mission. Mater politely turned them down. But he did take his spy gadgets for one last spin! Mater activated his rockets and blasted off down the racetrack, right beside his speedy best friend.